TOMMY BOMANI
Teen Warrior

Prophecy Fulfilled

BOOK 4

BY: Davy DeGreeff

magic
Wagon

visit us at www.abdopublishing.com

Thank you to my friends and family for all the help, support, and loving toleration of my unique personality—DD

Published by Magic Wagon, a division of the ABDO Group, 8000 West 78th Street, Edina, Minnesota 55439. Copyright © 2010 by Abdo Consulting Group, Inc. International copyrights reserved in all countries. All rights reserved. No part of this book may be reproduced in any form without written permission from the publisher.

Calico Chapter Books™ is a trademark and logo of Magic Wagon.

Printed in the United States.

Text by Davy DeGreeff
Cover art and chapter Illustrations by Sam Brookins
Edited by Stephanie Hedlund and Rochelle Baltzer
Cover and interior design by Jaime Martens

Library of Congress Cataloging-in-Publication Data

DeGreeff, Davy, 1984-
  Tommy Bomani : prophecy fulfilled / by Davy DeGreeff ; illustrated by Sam Brookins.
      p. cm. -- (Tommy Bomani, teen warrior ; bk. 4)
  Summary: Traveling to his ancestral home in Egypt to battle the evil wizard Badru, twelve-year-old Tommy Bomani, who has inherited great strength and an ability to shape-shift into powerful, large cats, must first find a missing piece of a statue carved by the Egyptian god Ra.
  ISBN 978-1-60270-700-9
  [1. Supernatural--Fiction. 2. Magic--Fiction. 3. Prophecies--Fiction. 4. Egypt--Fiction. 5. Youths' writings. 6. Youths' art.] I. Brookins, Sam, 1984- ill. II. Title. III. Title: Prophecy fulfilled.
  PZ7.D36385Tq 2009
  [Fic]--dc22
                                                          2009009463

Contents

Dreams

Tommy dug in the sand, pulled out the golden necklace, and placed it around his neck. It settled comfortably against his chest and filled his body with indescribable strength. He took a step back as a towering golden pyramid sprouted from the desert sand, perfect and new. With a smile, he began to climb.

The pyramid ledges were like giant steps, and Tommy made his way toward the top with ease. Along the way he found two more statue piece necklaces, identical to the one he wore. He placed them around his neck as well.

Tommy looked over his shoulder to the ground below. He saw his mother and his friends smiling and waving to him. He smiled and waved back.

He looked upward, to the peak of the pyramid. The sun rested directly over the top, like a beautiful crown, filling him with energy. He began to climb again. As he climbed, his legs started to tire and the three statue pieces grew heavy. He wondered if he would have enough strength to carry one more.

Tommy stopped and again looked toward the top. Although he had been climbing for a while, the peak didn't seem any closer.

Sweat trickled from his brow. He wiped it and noticed it was cold. He climbed some more, and then he stopped. He was breathing heavily now. Something in the air felt different. The day was still hot, but it seemed to be darker.

Tommy looked up again. The peak of the pyramid had disappeared, buried in a menacing black cloud. Tommy's mouth went dry. From within the cloud, a dark figure appeared.

It was Badru, floating down the pyramid in Tommy's direction. He was smiling, his teeth like daggers and his eyes burning like a midnight flame. He looked stronger than Tommy had remembered. Much stronger.

Without slowing, Badru flicked his wrist. The topmost necklace uncoiled itself from Tommy's neck. It flew straight into a hidden pocket in Badru's dark cloak.

Tommy felt like he was made of concrete, unable to move or react. Badru raised both hands and the second necklace removed itself from Tommy. It too made its way up the pyramid.

Badru stopped less than a yard from Tommy. He tilted his head back and laughed a deep, evil laugh that Tommy knew he had been holding for thousands of years. The sound of it sent shivers down Tommy's spine and rippled goose bumps on his arms.

Badru leaned forward and wrestled the final necklace from Tommy's neck. He placed it around his own neck, and with a self-righteous snarl he shoved Tommy backward.

Tommy didn't even bother to swipe at the empty air. He knew he had failed. He knew it was time for him to die.

He closed his eyes and listened to the desert wind whisper past his ears.

Houseguests

Tommy sat straight up in bed with a gasp, just as he had every morning for the past five days. He took a few deep breaths of hot desert air, wiped his long black hair from his eyes, and slammed a fist into his thin mattress. He was tired of being killed by Badru night after night.

Every night since they had landed in Egypt, the dream had been the same. It was worse than any other dream he had had in months. In fact, he hadn't had dreams this vivid since he had first discovered he could turn into a cat. That was also when he'd found out he was at the center of a war that had been raging for thousands of years.

Asim told Tommy that he was dreaming again because of the power this land held for him. Egypt was in his blood. This was where his family had begun. It was where he was tied to the people and the land and to the gods.

Asim assured him that there was nowhere else on Earth that Tommy's powers would be more active. And they would be especially strong now that he was wearing three pieces of the statue around his neck. It was expected that he would feel a little energetic, and that some of that extra energy would release itself in his dreams.

Tommy figured Asim had to be right. He'd never felt more restless in his life. Not even having Burt, Lily, and his cousin Annie in Egypt with him could distract him.

They had been in Egypt for almost a week, but all Tommy had seen of it was a dusty field where their private plane had landed. The Protectorate had provided the plane to help him on his mission, as they had for thousands of years. It was just too bad they had landed in the middle of the night and now had to hide inside a mud brick farmhouse.

The plan was to lay low for a day or two while Asim located Masud, an old friend of his who acted as a historian for the Protectorate. Masud could lead them to the sand-buried remains of the city where the Bomani bloodline had begun. Asim had hoped they would be able to find the last statue piece before Badru knew they had arrived.

So far their plan hadn't worked. Asim hadn't been able to find his friend. The man had completely disappeared. So now they were stuck in this farmhouse, unable to leave for fear that they would be recognized by one of Badru's spies. They wouldn't be able to move until Masud was found. As far as Tommy could tell, that might never happen.

Tommy sat up and rubbed his eyes. The sun hadn't even risen yet, but he knew he wouldn't be able to sleep. Once the dream came, any thoughts of sleeping went out the door.

Tommy looked over at Burt, who lay on the floor next to Tommy's bed. At least his best friend was able to get some sleep. Then again, that had never been a problem for Burt.

A quiet creak at the end of the small, boxy room stole Tommy's attention. The old wooden shutters swung inward very slowly. Quiet as a scorpion, someone began to crawl in the window.

"Another late night, Haji?" Tommy asked.

The boy in the window paused for a moment. Then, he continued climbing into the room and closed the shutters behind him. He ignored Tommy as he removed his dirty T-shirt and replaced it with another. Then he stepped over Burt and out the bedroom door.

"Good morning to you, too," Tommy muttered.

Haji was thirteen, a year older than Tommy, but a full inch shorter, with short-cropped black hair. The house belonged to Haji's family, and the bed Tommy was sleeping in was Haji's. Haji's grandmother had insisted that Tommy couldn't sleep on the floor and had forcefully offered her grandson's bed. Tommy had eventually accepted at Asim's urging, not wishing to appear rude.

Haji's family had served the Protectorate for generations and was immensely honored to assist Tommy in any way possible. Haji appeared to have some trouble falling in line with the rest of his family though. He was the only boy among four children, and he had made it clear from the beginning that he wasn't too pleased to share his room. He especially didn't want to share with someone his family treated like royalty.

Haji had slept on the floor of his own room for the first two nights. After that, he'd been sneaking out the window as soon as he thought Tommy and Burt were asleep. Tommy had caught him coming back in a couple of times. He had kept Haji's disappearances a secret, not wanting to push his thin relationship with the boy any further.

Tommy was grateful to the Nasif family for housing him and his friends, but he worried that they thought too much of him. Although he had plenty of time with nothing to do, he had not been allowed to help around the house at all. Haji's mother had explained that his godly blood made him too good for housework.

Tommy also began to notice a division within the house because of his presence. Haji's parents used Tommy as a shining example for everything, even if Tommy hadn't done anything special.

Tommy had begun to realize that if he were in Haji's shoes, he probably wouldn't want to share his bedroom either.

Tommy poked Burt with his toe and spoke softly. "Come on, buddy. Wakey, wakey. It's time to face another day."

CHAPTER 2

Breakfast

Burt followed Tommy into the main family room, where the rest of the household was already at the breakfast table. The sun was just beginning to peek through the open windows, but the smell of fava beans and flatbread opened Burt's eyes. Tommy drew back a seat between Annie and Asim.

Haji's mother, grandmother, and sisters were busy dishing food into bowls and placing them around the table. Asim and Mr. Nasif were bantering back and forth in Arabic. Burt took a seat next to Lily, who smiled and wished him a good morning.

Tommy ripped off a hunk of flatbread and leaned forward to dip it in the bean mixture sitting in front of him. Haji stretched across the table and slyly pulled the bowl toward himself without a word. With a forced polite smile, Tommy turned and took the bowl sitting in front of Burt. Burt was already too deep in conversation with Lily to notice anyway.

Tommy dipped his bread in the beans, took a large bite, and let out a satisfied groan. This trip to Egypt hadn't gone as planned so far, but one thing Tommy didn't regret was discovering a love for traditional Egyptian food. It was almost unbearable to think of going back to cheeseburgers when he returned home.

Finally the women sat down and began to eat as well. They talked a little, but mostly they did their best to enjoy the meal that would have to hold them over until suppertime.

Mr. Nasif was the first to get up from the table. He worked in the cotton fields and had to be at his post by sunrise. He made his way around the table but stopped to whisper something in Haji's ear. Haji made a disgruntled face, but Mr. Nasif nodded his head curtly, making sure Haji knew he had meant what he said.

Asim stood as well and readied himself to continue his search for Masud. He looked at Tommy and tilted his head to the side, indicating for Tommy to follow him.

Out of earshot from the others, Asim spoke in a low voice. "I know these days are long for you, Tommy. It won't be much longer, I promise you. I will find Masud. Until that time, you must be careful. Even more so than you have been."

"Is something wrong?" Tommy asked.

"I never thought it would take this long to locate Masud. He is elusive, but usually only to those he doesn't wish to find him. The way the people of this village are speaking when they answer my questions . . . I believe they are lying to me. Hiding something."

"I thought most of the people here served the Protectorate."

"Only a few decades ago that was certainly true. But as Badru's powers have grown, it seems that his influence over nearby areas has done the same."

Tommy thought about this. "But what does that have to do with Masud? Wouldn't he have told you if he left?"

"That is what I must discover, Tommy. We must hope that Masud is only missing, not gone." Asim grunted. "We may not be the only ones searching for him. You must do your best to make sure no one in the village realizes who we are. Right now our ability to claim the final piece of Ra's statue without Badru interfering rests completely with how well we keep you hidden. Do you understand?"

Tommy's eyes dropped to the ground. He wanted more than anything to charge out into the desert. But he knew Asim was right. They couldn't find the statue piece without Masud's instruction, and they'd never be able to find Masud if Badru found him first.

"Yes," Tommy finally responded.

Asim nodded and walked to the front door, which Mr. Nasif was holding for him. The men both stepped through and were gone.

Haji and his sisters stood from the table and gathered all the things they needed for their day at school. The girls kissed their grandmother's cheek and said good-bye. Haji kept quiet and shuffled away from the table. In a whirlwind they were out the door, escorted by Mrs. Nasif on her way to the marketplace.

And there they were again, left with Haji's grandmother for the fifth day in a row. Tommy, Annie, Burt, and Lily were stuck in a house next to the Egyptian desert with nothing to do but wait.

Tommy sighed and took another bite of bread.

CHAPTER 3

The Same, Everywhere

"**O**h, you're absolutely right! I've never even *considered* interpreting Descartes like that!" Burt gasped. He was sitting at the table with Lily, a pile of books between them.

"I told you, there's a lot more to French philosophy." Lily blushed, and then laughed at Burt. "Don't forget to breathe, Burt. I've got more where that came from." She laughed again and patted him on the shoulder.

Tommy watched them and smiled. Burt and Lily had sat at that table every day, all day since they had first touched down in Egypt. They discussed history, philosophy, battle strategy, poetry, and every other subject they were discovering a shared love for. It seemed like they barely even noticed that they were stuck inside just hoping Asim came home with the news that they would be able to move forward with their mission.

To say Tommy was jealous of their distraction was an understatement.

"Hey, cat food breath, you playing or what?" Annie said as she reached across the backgammon board to smack Tommy. That woke him up.

"Hey! Watch it, or I'm telling Asim we need to send you back to obedience school."

"Funny. Now you gonna go, or are you finally quitting and admitting that I'm way better than you?" Annie asked.

Tommy looked down at the game board, but the pieces swirled in front of his eyes. Since their first day in Egypt he and Annie had played backgammon, hoping it would help pass the time. But after more than a hundred games, Tommy almost felt ready to throw the board out the window and start banging his head against the wall. At least that would be a change of pace.

"Sorry Annie, I can't keep playing. I need a break," Tommy said.

"Works for me." Annie pushed away from the board and stretched out on the ground. She flashed back and forth between her dog form and her normal one. Then she yawned and walked to a pile of magazines she had managed to wedge into her suitcase.

"Hey Burt, what do you wanna bet I can get to the well and back in under a minute?" Tommy asked, interrupting Burt's conversation with Lily.

"I don't think that's such a hot idea, Tom. I'm guessing people would notice a panther running around in the middle of the day," Burt replied.

"Yeah, but if I take off the necklaces and just go as a normal house cat—," Tommy offered.

A growling sound from the corner stopped him. Haji's grandmother sat in a rocking chair fanning herself. The rumbling noise filling the room was definitely coming from her throat. She shook her head at Tommy.

As far as he knew, Haji's grandmother didn't speak a word of English. But every time Tommy suggested going outside, even just for a second, she made that horrible grinding noise. She was like Asim's permanent spy.

"Fine." Tommy threw up his hands. He sat down, but he couldn't stand playing even one more game. He rubbed his hands quickly around the board, thoroughly messing up the pieces and erasing any hint he and Annie had ever been playing.

"Looks like I win," Annie said, not looking up from her magazine.

"Whatever," Tommy replied. He glanced around, looking for anything that could potentially distract him. His eyes finally rested on the slight bulge in the front of his shirt created by the three mystical statue pieces.

Tommy took the necklaces off and held them before him. He moved them slightly from side to side and watched how the light danced on their golden surface. He concentrated on the power they sent surging through his body.

Tommy had definitely noticed a difference since he had taken to keeping all three necklaces near him. Everything he did was just a little smoother. They made him feel like anything was possible. But he had yet to see what their combined powers were truly able to do. Every time he even tried to imagine what abilities he might possess with the power of three statue pieces . . .

"Hey Tommy, would you give us a hand over here?"

. . . someone would cut in, perfectly on cue, with something that was sure to distract him until his urge to experiment had faded. Well, at least for the time being.

Tommy grudgingly tucked the necklaces back under his shirt. *We'll find out soon,* he promised himself as he walked toward Burt and Lily.

"What's up?" he asked.

Right as Lily opened her mouth to explain, the front door slid silently open. Haji stepped through, his face bruised and bloodied.

Haji's grandmother stood from her chair and shuffled quickly to Haji, who brushed her aside. He walked to the bathroom and emerged with a small towel held to his nose. His grandmother approached him again, speaking in rapid Arabic, trying to get a good look at his injuries.

The towel soaked up the blood from Haji's nose, but it did nothing for the bruise on his left eye. Tommy knew from experience that bruise would soon swell and turn purple.

Haji's mother and sisters came in through the open doorway. In a second his mother was standing next to his grandmother, repositioning the towel. With a frustrated yell, Haji broke free of them and ran into his bedroom. He slammed the door behind him.

Tommy looked to Mrs. Nasif, who had a resigned look on her face. She forced a smile and raised her hands in the air, palms up.

"Haji has problems with some boys from school. He is not strong and brave like you, Tommy Bomani, so they hurt him. He can do nothing to stop them," she said.

Tommy frowned. She was speaking as if Haji's problem with bullies was Haji's fault, like she was embarrassed of him. "I used to go through the same thing at school. It's not easy being smaller than everyone else."

Mrs. Nasif smiled and bowed her head. "Thank you, Tommy. But please do not make up stories to protect Haji. He is weak. It is something I accepted when he was very young."

"Does this happen often?" Burt asked.

"Often enough," Haji's mother responded.

Tommy shook his head, confused. The Nasifs had treated him and his friends with nothing but respect. But they did not hold the same respect for their own son.

Tommy knocked lightly on Haji's bedroom door, and let himself in when no response came.

"Haji?"

The boy was staring out the open window he had snuck in that morning.

"You should get something cold on your eye. It will take down the swelling a bit," Tommy suggested.

Haji ignored him. He continued to stare out the window. Tommy sat on the edge of the bed.

"You know, I used to have troubles with bullies a lot, too. I got beat up pretty much every week by these two idiots, Derrik and Shawn. They would terrorize me and would even push Burt around. I got more bloody noses than you could imagine."

Haji muttered something under his breath, in what sounded to Tommy like Arabic.

"What's that?"

Haji turned around. His eyes burned and there were tears in the corners. "Are you making fun of me, or do you really expect me to think you know what I go through every day? You have no idea what I go through. No idea."

"Haji, I—"

"What would you do when you got pushed around, Bomani?" Haji asked. "Would you go to your friends for protection? Or would you just turn into a panther and send the bullies running?"

Tommy paused, his mouth slightly open in confusion. "Haji, what are you talking about?"

The Egyptian boy stepped across the room and stopped in front of Tommy. He pointed a skinny, dirty finger in Tommy's face.

"Don't act like you know what it is to be powerless. You have had the power of the gods at your fingertips always. You have never been alone. Don't pretend to know what it's like to be me."

Tommy could see the tears that were ready to explode down Haji's cheeks. He couldn't think of what to say. He had no idea how to make Haji feel better or to make him understand that he wasn't as weak as everyone told him he was.

"You should really put a cool rag on that eye," Tommy said quietly.

"Get out of my room," Haji replied.

So Tommy did.

CHAPTER 4

Changing Times

A sim was the first person Tommy saw as he emerged from Haji's room. His mentor was speaking to Haji's father with a calm urgency. He waived Tommy over as soon as they made eye contact.

"Events have taken a turn I had hoped we would avoid, Tommy," Asim said. His voice was raspy, like he had been talking for an extended period of time.

"What's up?" Tommy asked. Annie, Burt, and Lily all surrounded him.

"While walking near the market I saw a woman I knew decades ago. She was never directly involved in the Protectorate, but I knew her to be honorable and reliable." Asim paused. He seemed to be shaping his words in his mind, to make sure he said what he wanted to say.

"When I saw that woman today, she was different. She was frightened, and she didn't trust me. It took me nearly an hour to convince her that I would not hurt her. When she finally confided in me, she told me what happened to Masud."

"Happened? Something happened to him?" Lily asked, wide-eyed.

"He has been kidnapped," Mr. Nasif stated.

"Apparently Badru has been hiring groups of thugs in all of the towns where he believes we may be hiding," Asim explained. "He has told them to search for us or anyone who may be assisting us. In exchange, Badru is offering the gangs a chance to loot the pharaoh's temple after the final statue piece is removed."

"And just like that people are willing to help him?" Lily asked.

"At least one gang, yes," Asim responded. "Word of Badru's presence spread, and Masud was forced into hiding. Nearly a week ago, a particularly vicious group of outlaws tracked Masud to a Protectorate household and stole him out in the dark of night. No one has seen him since."

"But you've talked to so many people," Tommy said. "How is this the first time you've heard of this gang?"

"The woman I spoke to said that they move Masud to a new location every few nights. But they tell witnesses that if they speak of what they've seen, their children will be killed and their houses burned to the ground."

Tommy looked out the hut's back window. The sun was setting, bringing another night without Masud and directions to the pharaoh's burial chamber. He shook his head. "I don't suppose the woman knows where they're keeping Masud?"

"No." Asim rubbed his temples and pushed out a quick sigh. "She told me she did not. But she assured me that even if she did know, she still wouldn't tell me. She very much believes that this gang would follow through on their threats."

"Everyone is evil until they're face-to-face with the biggest cat they've ever seen, right Tommy?" Annie said. "When do we get out there and start knocking on doors? I bet we could find them in one night, before they even knew we were looking."

"No. Not yet." Asim shook his head. "We don't know enough about them, so it would be too dangerous. Time is running short, but we must be patient and try to think of a wiser plan."

Tommy began to reply, but his words stopped short as he glanced out the window. His breath caught in his chest.

Tommy brushed past his friends as casually as he could to the other side of the room. He closed the window shutters and turned back around.

"So Asim, you're saying we're absolutely not searching for Masud tonight. Even though we know he's been kidnapped?" Tommy asked.

"I'm not saying that at all, Tommy. But I am saying that we must not barge out and expose ourselves like fools. It is not enough to be stronger than your opponent. You must also be wiser and more clever," Asim said.

Tommy yawned.

"Well, if we're not doing anything until after we eat, I'm going to take a quick nap," Tommy said.

"What? You were going bonkers all day because we didn't have anything to do. How could you possibly be tired?" Annie asked.

Tommy yawned again, more forcefully.

"I don't know. Just am, I guess. Maybe a little sleep will help me think of a plan. Who knows." Tommy shrugged. "Burt, will you wake me up when the food is ready?"

"Can do."

"Thanks." Tommy moved as calmly as he could to the bedroom door, then stretched one more time for emphasis. He stepped inside and shut the door behind him. Then, he glanced around the room.

Thought so. The room was empty. Haji was gone.

Tommy walked to the other end of the room. The wooden window slats looked closed, but with the slightest pull they swung in. He hoisted himself up into the window's brick opening and swung his legs through. Then, he dropped down into the darkened street and walked toward the narrow alley he had seen Haji run into.

Asim may not think we're ready to go into town, but I'm going crazy stuck in that house, Tommy thought. *I've got work to do. It looks like Haji has volunteered to be my tour guide.*

CHAPTER 5

An Ultimatum

Tommy peered down the alley. The houses in this small town were close together and made of a reddish brick, leaving very little light between them. He patted the statue pieces under his shirt for comfort and began moving forward.

The alley opened up into another dark lane, but this one was slightly larger and much longer. It ran alongside the backs of the neighboring houses and shops. Bottles lay on the ground and weeds grew in sparse patches through hard dirt. It was clear people rarely came back here. Tommy crouched low and made his way down the lane, looking for signs of Haji.

Tommy looked to his right and saw a flicker of movement. Across the street, a boy roughly Tommy's age and size crouched in the shadows outside an open window.

Haji.

Tommy stared, but couldn't quite make out what Haji was doing. The boy was kneeling on the ground, fumbling with something.

Tommy ran to the end of the alley and then slowed as he approached the street. It was dark but still light enough for someone to see his face if they got close enough. He glanced both ways and, convinced no one was watching, bolted across.

As Tommy was running, Haji lit a match and touched it to something that flared angrily. Tommy slid on the dirt into the alley like a baseball player, surprising Haji and causing him to drop what he had been holding.

"Haji!" Tommy whispered. "Whattaya say you show me around this charming little town of yours?"

Haji's eyes grew wide. He shook his head and flipped his eyes back and forth between Tommy and what he had dropped.

"Run!" Haji yelled and jumped past Tommy into the street.

Tommy looked down at a firecracker the size of his thumb, its fuse nearly burned to the base. He leaped frantically to his feet and chased after Haji.

A blast bellowed behind him as he turned into the street. For a brief second, fiery light lit the early night. Tommy followed Haji through an alley and behind a market cart. The boys crouched in the darkness and stared angrily at each other.

Lights began to turn on. Men stepped into the street to see what had happened. They couldn't see Tommy and Haji, so the boys stayed put.

"Where did you get that thing? You could have really hurt someone," Tommy whispered fiercely.

"He deserved what he had coming to him." Haji's eyes burned in the dark night. Tommy shuddered. The intensity in his eyes reminded Tommy of Marcellus Fisk.

"Not everyone can be a hero, Bomani, but that doesn't mean we can be stepped on. Some of us must just do what we can to fight back."

Tommy opened his mouth to respond, but he was never given the chance. The sky exploded into unnatural light fifty yards directly above them.

Badru appeared in the light.

The darkness of night was replaced by a glaring red light pouring from Badru. It was suddenly as bright as day, but the light felt menacing and invasive.

Badru raised his arms and spoke outward, not looking to any group in particular. His voice was hardly above a whisper, yet rang through the length of the town.

"You know who I am! You have heard my stories, and you have seen me in your dreams. I am the true pharaoh of these lands, and it is time you served me."

Those who had not been woken up by the exploding firecracker were awake now and were huddled near their doors. Children stayed close to their parents and all eyes were glued to the figure in the sky.

Badru was dressed in his standard black cloak, but it was in much better shape than the last time Tommy had seen him. There were no gaping holes, and the cloth looked nearly new. In fact, Badru himself looked stronger and more menacing.

He looks different than that hologram he sent of himself last time, Tommy thought. *I'm pretty sure that's actually him up there!*

Badru began to speak again. "There is an intruder in your midst, a false prophet. For centuries the Bomani bloodline has tricked you into serving the legacy of their fool pharaoh. But where is their pharaoh now? He is as dead as the gods who created the first Bomani. And now this young boy, the latest carrier of diseased Bomani blood, has entered your town without your knowledge. He seeks to raise the dead and steal from their tombs!"

Tommy's fists clenched. Badru was lying to bring people to his side. The people in the street began muttering amongst themselves and glanced around, as if hoping to catch Tommy sneaking through the night.

Tommy thought about stepping into the street and calling Badru out. Every version of the prophecy he had heard said that a final battle was inevitable, so why not get it over with now?

But then he took a breath and forced himself to consider things realistically. He had no plan, no support, and Badru had the advantage. For all he knew, the people in the streets believed Badru and would help him. It wouldn't work. Doing anything other than hiding for now would be too dangerous.

"Do not be fooled, my good people. Bomani cares nothing for you or for your country. He only wishes for the power to rule you. Help me find him and I promise you an eternity of riches."

Six unruly-looking men stepped out into the middle of the street. They were large, dirty, rough, and mean. Tommy knew in a second they had to be the men who had kidnapped Masud. He had no problem believing they would threaten to burn down someone's house and mean it.

Badru continued, "These are my servants. You are to report any suspicions you may have about Bomani's location to them. In return, they will ensure you are properly rewarded when we are victorious."

The gang began to walk down the street. Tommy watched as they scattered families like a bowling ball rolling a strike as they approached.

"Do not disappoint me, children," Badru boomed. His voice had taken on an extra edge of intensity and a snarl landed on his face. "If Bomani is not handed over to me in the next two days, I will assume you are hiding him. The punishment I bring will be severe."

In a blink, the darkness had returned and Badru was gone.

Tommy grabbed Haji by the hand and pulled him forward.

"Come on," he whispered. "If we don't get back, Asim is going to have another heart attack. Looks like Badru just pushed up our timetable."

They darted through the street and into the back alleys, perfectly covered by the dark blanket of night.

Visitors

Tommy slipped quickly in through the window and turned to help Haji step in. They closed the slats just as the bedroom door opened.

"Tommy? Did you see that?" Burt's voice was frantic. Lily and Annie followed him into the room.

"He knows we're here, Tommy. How is that even possible?" Annie said. She looked frightened. Tommy was used to her being so confident and aggressive, it was strange to see her so obviously upset.

"He's probably just guessing," Lily said. "I mean, he's gotta know we came to Egypt, right? He basically dared Tommy to come here when Fisk was arrested. And he knows this is where the last statue piece is. So if he just goes from town to town, doing the same thing, he's got to think that eventually he'll hit the right spot."

"A very good assumption, Lily." Asim stood in the doorway. "But we do not have the luxury of trusting assumptions right now. We must believe that Badru knows we have come for the piece, and we must act on that belief."

Tommy spoke, "Act how? We've been sitting in this house for almost a week. Without Masud . . ."

"The time has come to take more drastic actions," Asim replied. "Badru is becoming impatient. If he says he will begin harming the people of this town in order to find us, we must take his word."

"So what do we do? Start going door-to-door asking for Masud, hoping no one tells Badru? Asim, that doesn't make sense," Burt said. He sat down on the edge of the bed, clearly frustrated with the situation. "Now that we have an idea of what he's doing, I'm sure I can come up with a plan. I just need a little more time—"

"Time is one thing I am afraid we have spent too much of," Asim said, then he sighed. "You all know the story of the Abandoned City. As the crops began to fail, the Bomani children left their homeland and the great pharaoh died. This was when Bastet granted her descendants one last favor before she returned to the heavens. She buried their lifeless city in a great sandstorm to protect it from those who would pillage and dishonor its remains."

Tommy picked up the story. "The city will only rise from the sand one more time, and only for a Bomani. Badru knows this. He knows I'm the only chance he has of ever reaching the final statue piece."

"Precisely." Asim nodded. "He believes you know where the city is buried. If Badru were to discover that you do not know the statue's location, it would give him all the power. I am sorry I wasted so much time believing I could find Masud on my own. Children, I need help from all of you."

Asim looked to Haji, who avoided eye contact. "We must work together to find him, so he can lead us to the pharaoh's tomb before Badru is able to locate us."

Burt stood from the bed, confusion on his face. "But Asim, if Badru knows we're here, and if his prophecy is correct—"

Burt's words were cut short by a fist slamming against the front door. Asim's eyes went wide, and he quickly pulled the bedroom door shut, closing the other five in darkness. Tommy heard him whisper to them harshly from the other side.

"Stay here and do not make a sound."

Tommy heard the front door open, followed immediately by heavy footsteps marching in.

Mr. Nasif spoke to whoever had entered. A man yelled his response, and the men with him laughed. Tommy heard one of Haji's sisters shriek, and the men laughed louder.

Asim barked something at the men. Everything being said was in Arabic, but Tommy could tell from the tone of Asim's voice that he was angry. There was a brief, silent pause when he finished.

A flash of movement against the dim light of the window caught Tommy's eye. He looked up just in time to see Haji sneak out into the night once more. Tommy shook his head and turned his attention back to the action on the other side of the door. Haji would have to be on his own this time.

Tommy slipped past Burt and cracked open the door ever so slightly. Three large men stood in the doorway. Tommy recognized them as members of Badru's gang. Asim stood in front of them, the only barrier between the Nasif family and the intruders.

The largest of the men, who Tommy assumed was the leader, shoved his finger in Asim's face and spoke in a scraping whisper. His face was turning red. Apparently he hadn't liked what Asim had said.

The man pointed to the sky and then to the ground. When Asim responded with only a shake of his head, the man became even more enraged.

He took two steps to the side and punched a hole straight through the wall. Haji's mother nearly fell to the ground in fright, but her husband caught her. The family grouped closer together.

A large hand wrapped itself around Tommy's mouth as another pulled him back, and Lily silently closed the door. When he was sure Tommy wouldn't yell, Burt let go of him. Tommy slipped forward and rested his ear against the door.

The angry man began speaking once more, again in a harsh whisper. Haji's father responded weakly. The angry man grunted.

Tommy heard heavy steps shuffle away, and eventually the door shut. He stepped back from the bedroom door.

Asim pushed the bedroom door open. His face was a blank slate. "You must all do your best to get some sleep. Tomorrow we must find Masud. Those men offered a reward for information regarding Tommy's location. They said that if Tommy is not brought to them within the next two days, this is the first home they will destroy."

"If they try, we'll fight them," Tommy said.

Annie joined in. "Yeah, let them try."

Asim shook his head. "Fighting them would

only reveal our position to Badru. As soon as night fell he would be sure to attack."

"But if he kills Tommy, he won't be able to get to the last piece of the statue," Annie said.

"Unfortunately, you and I are not as necessary for his plans, Ms. Wolfe. He would surely use us to force Tommy to do his bidding," Asim replied.

"Do we have any idea where to begin?" Burt asked.

Asim laughed humorlessly. "Right now we are left with no other plan than to rise early and search as frantically as we can. We must hope that our luck is stronger than that of our enemies."

"You told me luck only exists as an excuse for those who don't know how to win," Tommy said.

Asim nodded. "So let us hope that inspiration strikes you in the night, Tommy. So we are not left to such a foolish guide as fate."

CHAPTER 7

Night Hunt

Tommy lay flat on his back and stared up to the ceiling. Everyone had retired to their rooms just over an hour ago, but Tommy felt more awake than he had all day. His mind kept racing, running over all the possibilities the next day could hold.

Is this the beginning of the prophecy coming true? he thought. Tommy still hadn't decided if he believed the stories of Badru's fortune-telling dreams. But he couldn't imagine a way the next day or two *wouldn't* lead to a battle between himself and his family's worst enemy.

If they were able to locate Masud and then the statue piece, the next logical step would be to attack Badru to take the remaining pieces. And if they didn't find Masud and Badru began punishing innocent people, Tommy would be forced to challenge Badru, whether he felt ready to or not.

And I should feel ready, shouldn't I? he thought. He had never felt more powerful or capable in battle. He was sure that having more than one piece of the statue with him must somehow increase his powers. But in what way?

Since he had begun wearing all three pieces it seemed like they sang to him. They were begging him with a near-silent hum to let them show just how powerful their combined forces could make him. Yet every time he had even tried imagining what more he could possibly be capable of, something would interrupt him.

He was supposed to challenge the most dangerous man in the history of civilization to mortal combat and he didn't even know what would happen when he changed shapes.

None of his ancestors had ever changed shapes powered by more than one piece. How should he know what to expect? And how would his powers be affected by the fact that he carried Wolfe blood as well? Didn't some of the prophecy interpretations say that would change his abilities in unexpected ways?

Tommy sat up in bed, his head spinning. He was gripping the necklaces with both hands and pulled them from his neck. He *had* to know what they would make him capable of. He had to know how strong he would become.

Tommy stared straight forward and concentrated on the power pulsing from the necklaces. He took a deep breath—and fate intervened again, forcing him to wait just a little longer.

Wood creaked quietly and dull light flooded the other end of the room. Tommy quickly placed the necklaces back over his head and watched Haji slip in through the window.

Haji made his way through the dark room. He soon stood in front of Tommy. He was breathing heavily and he looked upset.

"Thank goodness you're awake," Haji said, not bothering to whisper. "You must wake everyone you will need, Bomani, and act quickly."

"What are you talking about?" Tommy asked. Adrenaline began pumping into his veins.

"I have found the man you are looking for. He is in trouble. If you want to help him, we must go now."

Tommy looked into Haji's eyes, and then leaped from the bed. He nudged his sleeping friend as he sped by.

"Wake up, Burt," he hollered on his way out of the room. "Our work day is starting early."

Haji, Tommy, Burt, Lily, Annie, and Asim huddled close together in the darkness behind the house. All of them except Asim had snuck to the back through Haji's window, hoping they could avoid arousing the suspicions of the neighbors. The surrounding houses all rested peacefully unaware.

"You must all follow me closely and be prepared to fight or run as soon as I give the word," Haji whispered. "I followed those men after they left my house. They went to a building on the edge of town that hasn't been used in years. I saw them standing around an old man tied to a chair. He looked tired, like they had been hurting him."

"And you're sure it's Masud?" Asim asked.

Haji shrugged. "I couldn't be positive, I've only met him once before, but . . ."

"What better lead do we have?" Tommy finished. "Lead the way, Haji. Getting Masud out of there is just the beginning of our day. We need to get started. Annie, why don't you bring up the rear?"

Annie changed shapes and immediately began wagging her shaggy brown tail. Tommy's statue pieces warmed against his chest, as if jealous. He did his best to ignore the sensation.

Haji looked to Annie, then to Tommy, and then to Asim. He was beyond confused.

"Have your parents never told you? The Bomanis are not the only family with remarkable talents. Now come, time is wasting," Asim demanded.

Haji let out a long breath and paused, as if he were deciding something. Finally, he turned and began to creep along the brick wall. The group followed him down the same thin alleyway he and Tommy had run through earlier that night.

They darted and weaved through a number of alleys. Tommy was grateful that Haji had made a conscious effort to keep them from being seen. It seemed as if Haji's opinion toward them had shifted after seeing Badru. His willingness to help couldn't have come at a better time.

After about ten minutes of crouching, slinking, and sprinting through shadows, Haji held up his hand and peered around a corner. He turned and signaled for everyone to stay put and then darted across a large open patch of sand to a worn building. He grabbed the edge of a wooden window shutter and slowly pulled it back.

A sliver of light poured onto his face as he peered inside. He cautiously let the shutter fall back against the building and waved the rest of the group over. Tommy led the way, checking in every direction as they moved. Annie came to the building last, and with a nod from Tommy, she shifted back into her normal form.

Haji sparked his lighter to illuminate his face. He whispered, "The old man is inside, and so are all six men. They're all asleep."

"I think we should sneak in and get Masud out before they even know he's gone," Lily said.

"Where's the fun in that?" Annie asked, smiling. "While we're here we might as well take down some thugs."

Tommy smirked at Annie's enthusiasm. "Sorry Annie, but Lily's right. The quicker we're in and out, the quicker we're on our way to the Abandoned City. An unnecessary fight would take up too much time."

Annie shrugged. "You're the boss."

Tommy turned to Asim and continued to whisper, "You want to plan this one?"

"I can counsel if you need it, but this is your adventure now, Tommy."

"Okay then. I'll lead and Annie, you take the rear again. Haji, follow right behind me. We'll go in and pull Masud out. Burt, I want you right by the door in case something goes wrong and you need to rush in. Lily, stick close to Asim and keep your eyes open for anything we might miss."

Tommy took a deep breath and let it out slowly. "Ready team? Let's get this done."

They crept along the front of the building in the order Tommy had decided until they reached the door. Tommy twisted the knob and grimaced as the rusty metal scratched out a high-pitched tune. Then, he slowly pulled the door outward.

Without warning a hand shoved the middle of his back, forcing him forward. He instinctively brought a hand to his eyes to shield the sudden light. Then he ducked at the sound of the door slamming shut behind him.

CHAPTER 8

Fooled

On pure instinct, Tommy shifted shapes and moved to the corner of the room. This covered his rear and gave him a full view of the room in front of him.

Haji had been right. And he had been very, very wrong.

Masud was tied firmly to a wooden chair in the middle of the large, open room. Empty bottles and trash was spread all around the floor. There were sleeping bags and blankets in crumpled piles scattered in no particular pattern.

But the bags were empty.

None of Badru's men were in the building.

Tommy changed back to his regular form and tried the door he had been pushed through. It rattled a little, but wouldn't budge. Someone must have blocked it from the outside.

Tommy rushed to Masud. The old man's eyes were open, but he hardly seemed conscious.

"Masud?" Tommy asked.

He nodded, barely. Masud was bruised on every inch of his weathered face. His lips trembled as he formed one word: "Trap."

Tommy grabbed both of his frail shoulders. "Don't worry, I'm going to get you out of here."

A scream came from outside. Tommy looked back to Masud.

"Hold still, I'll get these ropes off of you. And then stay here. I'll be back in a minute." Tommy changed shapes and slashed the ropes into ribbons. Masud rubbed his wrists and thanked him.

Tommy looked around the room, but the locked door was the only one he could find. Then he saw the window that Haji had peeked in and bolted toward it.

He exploded through the window, sending the wooden shutters through the air in a stupendous volley of rotting splinters. His wide body narrowly scraped through the sides.

Tommy skidded on the loose dirt and did his best to take in the scene before him. Burt and Annie stood next to him, against the wall. Annie was in dog form, and Burt had his hands in tight fists, bobbing through the air. Forty yards away Badru's gang was loading Lily and Asim into a pair of pickup trucks. One of the six men was sitting in the back of the front truck, pointing a rifle straight at Burt.

In between the two groups, sprawled on the ground, was Haji. His nose was bleeding once again.

Burt hardly seemed to notice that Tommy had arrived. "Put the gun down and fight us, you cowards!" he screamed.

Near the second truck, the leader shoved Asim into the backseat. Then he turned to Burt with a smile.

"Try to follow us and your girlfriend won't be the only one who dies. And thank you for the help, Haji. I'm sorry our relationship wasn't quite what you expected it to be." The man banged twice on the side of the truck and jumped into the open truck bed as both vehicles sped off toward the desert.

Tommy and Annie gave chase, but it wasn't long before the trucks' engines outmatched their legs. They stopped and watched as the taillights disappeared over a sand dune and into the darkness.

Grudgingly, they turned back toward the building and ran. When they arrived, they found

Burt kneeling over Haji, his hands wrapped firmly around the boy's neck.

Tommy and Annie switched back to human form as they ran, but only Tommy screamed for Burt to stop. From ten yards away he raised his arm in Burt's direction and felt a surge of heat pulse from the statue pieces to ends of his fingers. As if a large wind had hit him square in the chest, Burt toppled backward to the ground.

Tommy stopped short, his eyes wide.

Annie and Burt stared at him. Haji rubbed his throat and coughed, then scrambled to his feet and began to run. Annie snapped from her trance and chased him, tackling him to the ground and pinning him in place.

Tommy shook his head, trying to match up all that had happened in the past two minutes. His thoughts swirled like smoke through his mind.

"Annie . . . ," Tommy said, walking toward her, slowly. "Let him up."

"Don't! Annie, hold him there!" Burt yelled. He blasted past Tommy and stopped with his finger pointed inches short of Haji's face. Blood still flowed freely from his nose to his chin.

"He betrayed us, Tommy," Burt continued.

"And now they have Lily and Asim!" Burt's face was beet red. Not only had Tommy never seen him this angry, but before now he couldn't have imagined his friend even capable of becoming this enraged.

Tommy stopped and stared at the three people in front of him, barely visible in the night.

"What do you mean he betrayed us? How?" Tommy asked.

"I'm so sorry, Bomani. I didn't . . . I didn't think they would . . . ," Haji started, but his words turned to tears and sobs. He hung limply in Annie's grip.

"Haji is friends with Badru's thugs, Tommy," Annie said. "He led us here so they could bring you to Badru."

"Is that true, Haji?" Tommy asked. His heart was pounding his rib cage into splinters.

Haji stared at the ground. "The old man told them where the Abandoned City is. He drew them a map earlier. They said they wanted to raid it before Badru knew anything. But when I said I knew where you were, they decided they could make double their money. They were going to raid the ruins and then sell you to Badru before he realized what they had done. I can't believe, I . . ."

Haji continued crying. His body shook.

"They obviously don't know they can't get to the Abandoned City without Tommy," Annie said.

Tommy tried to move closer, but it felt as if there were an invisible object between himself and Haji, forcing them apart.

"Did those men give you that gigantic firecracker, Haji?"

Haji nodded.

"What else did they promise you, once you said you knew where I was?"

"Anything. Everything. They said they would share the loot they stole from the ruins. They said my parents wouldn't have to be poor anymore. They said my sisters could afford new clothes every school year. But they lied. Why? Why would they do that?" Haji bellowed.

"Because they're criminals," Annie said.

"We have to go after them, Tommy. We have to get Masud to draw us the same map he drew for them," Burt said.

"Masud!" Tommy slapped his forehead and then ran his fingers through his hair.

"We've got to find them, Tommy, before they do something to Lily," Burt urged. "Please."

Tommy thought for a second, then nodded. "You're right. There's nothing else here for us now. Doing our best to get to the temple before they do is our strongest bet."

Annie pushed Haji back to the ground and joined Burt and Tommy in walking to the building's door. Tommy now saw that it was held shut with a large, heavy tire.

"Wait!" Haji yelled behind them. Tommy stopped, but the other two continued, deaf to his voice. "Let me come with you!"

Tommy turned away from him and continued walking.

"Please! Let me repay what I have done. Let me redeem myself."

Tommy looked to Haji once more, who was on his knees, begging.

"Two of my best friends might die tonight because of you. You might have cost us any advantage we ever held over Badru. I think you've done enough for tonight," Tommy said, and turned his back on Haji for the final time.

CHAPTER 9

No Time to Waste

They found Masud slumped in his chair, asleep with one of the blankets wrapped around him. Tommy shook his shoulder gently. "Masud? Sir?"

The old man snapped awake and recoiled with his hands in front of his face. When he saw that it was only the children, he let out a defeated sigh and rubbed his eyes.

"I can't believe I fell asleep, but . . . I am truly exhausted. I see you have saved your friends. That is good. Then there can be no doubt that you are a Bomani. I had hoped you would come soon." His voice was raspy and dry, and his accent sounded exactly like Asim's, rich and guttural.

"We didn't save all of them. We need your help. Badru's gang kidnapped Asim and our friend Lily and put them in trucks heading for the desert," Tommy said.

Masud rose slightly in his seat. "Asim? He is here?"

"He's been looking for you for a week," Burt said.

"Do you think you could give us the same map you gave those men? The map to the Abandoned City?" Tommy asked.

"Well, which would you like? The map I gave those men or the map to the Abandoned City?" Masud responded, smiling broadly.

"What?" Annie asked. "Are you messing with us?"

"Not at all, dear, not at all." Masud smiled again, and accepted a bottle of water Burt had found in a corner of the room. He took a long drink, draining the whole bottle. "Thank you, son. You see, children, those men did not capture me on accident. From the first day they abused me, hoping I would tell them the location of the Pharaoh's Tomb. I held out for what felt like weeks, but finally I drew them a map earlier today."

"Why did you give in?" Burt asked.

"Because I knew help was coming. I knew you wonderful people were nearby. This land is thick with mystery, children. But in our worst time of need, a Bomani warrior will arrive to shed light on a dark day." Masud began to stand. He concentrated on making sure each limb still worked.

"Well, if you knew we were coming, why did you draw them a map? Doesn't that kind of defeat the purpose?" Annie said.

Tommy answered. "He said he drew them a map, but he didn't say it was to the tomb."

Masud clapped a hand on Tommy's back. For a frail old man, he packed a powerful swing. "Exactly! Now let's get going! Time is never our friend, and tonight it may very well be our enemy." He began to walk to the door.

Burt held fast. "But where are we going? No way we're just leaving Lily and Asim with those men."

"I wouldn't dream of it. That is why we must find a ride into the desert. Even the shortest of shortcuts must be traveled, and I fear that my old bones wouldn't take me too far if we were to try walking," Masud said. Then he turned on his heel back toward the door. "Come, quickly. I know just the place to find some excellent camels."

Masud's Wisdom

Burt held a hand to his mouth. His face was green even in the pale rising sunlight. His camel moved with halting shrugs across the desert sand, bringing Burt closer to throwing up with each step.

The temperature rose by the minute. Tommy wiped the sweat from his forehead. He had already tied his long, black hair back into a pathetic ponytail with a rubber band Annie had found in her pocket. *Anything to keep it out of my face,* he thought.

Annie led the way by a quarter mile, but against the open layout of the desert she was still easily visible. She was desperate to reach the battleground, and her hunger for confrontation didn't hide itself well.

Burt was just as anxious to take revenge against the men. But he hung back with Tommy and Masud, hoping they would spend the trip planning.

But to this point, no one had said a word.

Finally, Masud broke the silence.

"It had been a dark time before you arrived, Tommy Bomani," he said. "The time since your father's death . . . it has not been a good one for the Protectorate."

"How can that be? According to Asim, Tommy's family has always protected the people from Badru. The people have served the Protectorate because they knew that it stood for what was right, not because they felt they had to. Why would they stop believing the Bomanis would protect them?" Burt asked.

Masud shrugged. "Times change. People change. They saw that Badru was growing stronger and that their last hopes were in the hands of a child. They began to cast their bets with the team they thought might have the best chance to win. People are wired to do what they think is best for their own future."

"It doesn't seem right. Tommy's family worked hard for them. To leave the Bomanis without giving Tommy a chance to prove he's worthy . . ." Burt tossed his hands into the air. "I just know I couldn't do it."

"Not everyone is as strong as you are, Burt," Masud said. "Badru's grip may have increased, but there are still many who oppose him. I never lost faith. The Nasifs never lost faith, at least for the most part. And the man who gave us these camels? Children, he isn't even a member of the Protectorate.

"He was once a great man in our village. He threw it all away when he saw that he had gained his riches by unknowingly serving Badru's will. He moved into a hut that would have fit into the bathroom of his former home, because he knew that all the riches in the world couldn't make him feel proud of having served such an evil man."

Masud pulled the reins on his camel, and Burt and Tommy did the same. They stood together as a tiny, dark splotch in the gigantic sea of sand.

"The names of the Nasifs and the man who gave us these camels will be lost to time, Tommy. That is inevitable. But your name must not be lost. If the decency of humanity is to continue, you must be remembered as the hero who saved us all. When the time comes, you must do whatever is necessary to secure the statue pieces. Sacrifice anything if it means you can disrupt the prophecy."

Tommy gripped his camel's reins. "I thought that prophecies were unbreakable. Badru has seen the future and has seen himself with the statue pieces. Doesn't that mean it's meant to happen, regardless of what I do?"

Masud laughed. His laugh melted into the swirling winds that were rising and pelting their skin with bullets of sand. "If you really thought that was true, Bomani, would you be marching through the heat of the desert alongside me, intent on fighting a battle you were destined to lose?"

Tommy said nothing. He heeled his camel forward.

"I thought not, Tommy Bomani," Masud said. "I thought not."

The shape of Annie lying pressed to the top of a sand dune slid into focus as they grew nearer. She had left her camel behind and dropped flat onto her stomach, staring over the peak.

Tommy steered his camel next to hers and dropped to the ground. Burt turned his steed in the same direction, but slowly rolled out from between its humps. He was still queasy from the uneven ride.

Burt and Tommy crouched next to Annie and lay down on either side of her. She didn't react to their presence.

Tommy opened his mouth to ask what she was looking at and stopped short.

What looked like a small dune was actually the beginning of a drop-off to a rolling hill. At the base was a great series of windswept ruins, and in the middle of the ruins were two rusted pickup trucks.

Asim sat next to the trucks, his wrists tied together and a cloth bag over his head. He was alone.

"Where's Lily?" Burt asked. Panic was already in his voice.

Tommy used his already-damp T-shirt to wipe his forehead. It was late afternoon and they were tired, hungry, and overheated to the point of desperation. He couldn't imagine what it felt like for Asim to be sitting directly in the sun with a heavy cloth bag blocking his fresh air.

"Where are the men?" Tommy asked. "That's what we need to figure out before worrying about Lily."

"There." Annie pointed to a large, rectangular hole in the ground. Shining white walls stuck partially out of the sandy floor. A group of shovels, sacks, flashlights, and various other tools lay on the ground near the hole. "They must be inside trying to find the treasure."

Masud walked up behind them. He snickered. "But there is none to find. I chose these ruins because they are close and because they are picked clean of valuable items. Those bandits should keep digging for hours before getting frustrated enough to realize they've been fooled."

"How long would you guess they've been in there?" Burt asked.

"Oh, I gave them a roundabout sort of route. I'd say they probably arrived here two or three hours ago."

"Then we'd better get to work. They're not going to be happy campers when they crawl out of that empty hole," Tommy said, standing up. "Burt, you're on, buddy. What kind of plan is brewing in that big ol' brain of yours?"

CHAPTER 11

Realized Potential

"**H**ere! I'm over here!" Asim yelled. "Help me!"

"Be quiet, Asim. The men will hear you yelling," Burt said back loudly, and then whispered. "Thanks Asim. Just give me a second, I'll get these ropes off you. Then the show starts . . ."

Burt worked clumsily to untie the ropes that held Asim's hands behind his back. Masud pulled the bag from around his friend's face. Asim pulled in a heaving breath. His hair was wet with sweat and strands clung to his forehead like limp spaghetti noodles. Masud laughed loudly.

"We have done it, friend! We have freed you!" Masud hollered, and immediately regretted not checking the volume of his voice.

"Hey!" a man yelled at them from the mouth of the ruins. He stood half in and half out of the ground, his face smeared with dirt. He yelled in Arabic and charged at them, a shovel in his hand.

He ran in a straight line to Burt and pulled the shovel back, ready to swing. Burt dropped to the ground and threw his arms in front of his face.

"Oh!" Burt yelled. "Please don't hurt me! Asim, run! Run, Masud!"

But the man didn't follow through on his threat. Instead he aimed the shovel at the two older men, forcing them on the ground next to Burt. The man ran back to the opening in the ground and yelled a warning in Arabic.

Within moments the rest of his men had joined the fray.

They all held makeshift weapons of wood and metal. Less than ten feet from where Burt lay, one of them suddenly stopped the rest with a series of low, barked orders. He looked around suspiciously. The rest of the men followed suit and began to look to the corners of the abandoned buildings and piles of rubble.

They were right to be suspicious.

From around a freestanding ancient wall charged an angry gray bull the size of a small tank. It blasted straight through the middle of the group, taking two men with it, one on each horn. It had hooked them each under the armpit and tossed them headfirst into a pile of loose stone, where they stayed.

The rest of the men tried to scramble away, but a large, shaggy dog leaped out from behind a lonely pillar. It herded them back to a tight group with barks and well-placed bites. One took a swing at it and found the wooden staff he had tried to use as a weapon torn right from his hand.

The bull reeled around and made another pass. This time it managed to throw the largest of the three remaining men straight up in the air. He came down hard inside the metal bed of one of the trucks.

The men split up and ran in opposite directions. The dog gave chase to one, biting at each heel as it kicked up from the sand. The man swatted helplessly behind him, but he simply couldn't outrun his pursuer. Frantic and desperate, he leaped into a ring of stone and dropped out of sight.

Annie skidded to a stop and transformed into her regular self. She looked down into the well the man had jumped into. He stood on the dry bottom, at least ten yards underground, with no means of climbing out.

The man looked to Annie and yelled at her. He began to claw at the dirt walls but only made it up a few feet before falling back down.

"Sorry," she yelled down to him. "I can't understand you. Hold on, I'll go see if I can get one of your friends to translate." She smiled and clapped her hands together, then she shifted back and ran toward the fight.

The last man decided to stand his ground. He held a heavy shovel and stared at the bull, which stood twenty yards away, running a hoof through the dirt and snorting.

The bull took off, but the man didn't flinch. He tightened his grip on the shovel's shaft and raised it level with his shoulder, ready to strike. The bull grew closer and closer. The man's jaw grew slack as he realized how freakishly large the beast was, but still he kept from running.

The bull's hooves beat against the ground like thunder, shaking every brick and pebble. At the halfway point it began to shrink and thin, and its horns started to recede into the thick, gray skin that was quickly beginning to resemble glossy, silver hair.

The man trembled, but he did not break.

The bull took two more steps and was a bull no more, its transformation complete. It was now an enormous panther. It leaped through the air like a silver demon, planting himself inches from the man's face. It let out a growl so forceful the man's hair fluttered. His eyes twisted shut, his head bobbled slightly on his neck, and he slowly passed out from sheer fright.

Tommy turned and looked to Asim, who was shaking his head in wonder.

"Tommy, I . . . that was *amazing*."

Annie was clapping her hands. "That was awesome! Imagine what you could do with all of the pieces!"

Burt opened his mouth, but the next voice didn't belong to him.

"Yes, yes, yes, all very impressive. You should use those mixed-blood powers to find my treasure. Now! Or she dies!"

All heads turned to the mouth of the ruins. There the last of Badru's men was standing with Lily, a knife held firmly to her throat.

CHAPTER 12

From the Shadows

The man shuffled forward. Lily was gagged with a dirty rag, and her tears had traced lines down her dirt-caked cheeks.

"Change back. Now!" the man yelled. He was the leader of the gang, the one who had yelled at Asim the night before. He had been hiding in the shadows of the temple ruins, waiting to see if his men won or lost.

What a coward, Tommy thought as he changed back to his normal form. "There, I changed back. Now give us Lily."

The man barked a laugh. His eyes were dark slits, which stayed glued to Tommy. "I'm no idiot. I have heard the legends of your family. This girl is my only way out of here."

"That's not true," Burt said. Annie had a hand on his chest, trying to keep him from charging forward. "There is no way out for you. If anything happens to her, we will hunt you. And then you'll pay."

"Haji had told me you were the quiet one. He said you'd go down without a fight. It looks like I've found your soft spot." The man snarled and twisted his knife. Lily tensed and Burt clenched his fists, but he was too far away to do anything. "Of course, Haji also neglected to mention that the witch next to you can turn into a hound, so it may just be that Haji didn't know what he was talking about."

Somehow Lily managed to spit the rag from her mouth. "Stop, Burt. He'll hurt you. Tommy needs you to help find the statue."

"Yes, Burt, your friend needs you. Don't do anything stupid." The kidnapper took a step to the side, toward the trucks. He looked at Masud. "Old man, be glad this it isn't you under my blade. Today was supposed to be the day I became rich, and you made me nothing but a fool."

Masud smiled, large and genuine. "And it hardly took any work at all."

The man spit at him. "We'll meet again, and at that time you'll eat that smile."

The man took another step. He was only a few feet from the trucks.

"Where do you think you're going?" Tommy asked.

"Once my new little friend and I are in my truck, you mean? I'm not sure, but you will never find me. This is my country, child. Your kind left long ago. Once I'm over that hill, you'll never see me again. I didn't get my treasure, but I'm not going away with nothing."

"Tommy . . . ," Lily said, trembling. "I'm so sorry. I hope you find the last piece. I—I'm so sorry."

Tommy could feel the last rays of the sun hitting the back of his neck as it dropped toward the horizon. In a few minutes it would be completely dark. This stalemate had to end before that happened, but he couldn't risk shifting. It just wouldn't be fast enough.

"Stop," Tommy said.

But the man took another shuffled step and pulled Lily tighter to him. "I don't take requests from spoiled children."

Tommy closed his eyes in concentration. "That wasn't a request."

The trucks began to vibrate and then shake. The bandit whipped his head back and forth between them and Tommy, unsure what was happening.

Everyone else did the same. Tommy stayed still, his eyes pressed together.

Sand rose from the ground and whipped around the vehicles in a growing tornado. Lily held her bound hands over her eyes. The dirt-covered criminal stared at Tommy. He kept the knife to Lily's throat, his thick tattooed arm unmoved. His dirty, black hair snapped harshly in the wind.

"It isn't working, Bomani!" he yelled above the sandstorm. "Your tricks aren't impressing me! You can't win."

The tinging of sand on metal melted into a deep groaning, like the trucks were being bent slowly against their will. Suddenly, the ground beneath them opened up and swallowed them entirely.

The wind stopped and the sand ceased flying. Seconds ago there were two pickup trucks, but now there was a patch of sand no different than the ones stretching for miles around.

The man breathed heavily, panicking. His eyes darted from side to side, resting back on Tommy every few seconds. He took a step backward, and then another two.

"You aren't going anywhere. Now let the girl go," Tommy said. His voice was calm and even.

The man mumbled in Arabic and spit on the ground. He took another step back and pulled Lily tight against him. She had begun crying again.

"Please," Tommy said again. "I don't want to hurt you. Just let her go and you're free to walk back to town."

The man froze. His eyes stopped darting and locked on Tommy's. He growled, showing his teeth like an animal, and shook his head from side to side.

His body went tight, and he dropped the knife.

The bandit fell over, dead.

CHAPTER 13

Inevitable Beginning

L ily ran forward and jumped into Burt's arms. He embraced her, but he was staring at Tommy in shock. So was Asim.

"Tommy . . . what have you done?" Asim asked. "Is he—did you kill him?"

Tommy shook his head and looked past Asim. The sun was minutes from disappearing, and Tommy used the last remaining light to walk over to his friends. "No, that wasn't me. I don't know what it was."

But he did know what it was. He just didn't know how that could be. There was only one person he could think of with the ability to kill a man without laying a hand on him.

"I killed that rat," Badru said as he marched between two half-destroyed ruins. "Your child warrior doesn't have the fortitude to take another man's life. He is a watered-down version of every pathetic Bomani before him."

Annie shifted immediately to her dog form and began growling. Lily slid behind Burt's large frame. Masud and Asim climbed to their feet, ready to fight tooth and nail.

Badru walked coolly, like he knew exactly where he was going and had all the time in the world to get there. The sun had now dropped from view, but he was perfectly visible in the dark. His cloak hung loosely, but he looked strong and tall. His head was shaved and a thin beard wound to a point below his chin.

But Tommy noted that he also looked old and tired. Badru stopped twenty yards away, his arms crossed in front of his chest.

Tommy took a few steps forward. He kept his knees flexed, ready to jump into action if necessary. He did his best to look calm and confident.

"How did you find us? I thought your men were making this trip behind your back." Tommy smirked, but his lip quivered slightly. Adrenaline kicked into his veins, reminding him that he was about to enter the most important fight of his life.

"There is nothing in my kingdom I do not see. These men were fools to think they could trick me."

Tommy ran his hands through his hair. "So I suppose you came here to fight, then. To see if your prophecy was correct." Tommy licked his suddenly dry lips. "I'm ready when you are, old man."

"You only breathe because I don't wish you to suffocate, child. At least not yet," Badru said. "Before you are worthy enough for me to take your life, you must do one last thing. There is still a final statue piece to be recovered, and I cannot gain access to it without your wretched bloodline."

"So you expect me to find the Abandoned City, retrieve the piece, and hand it over to you?"

"You have no choice. Without a fourth piece, you have no hope of overpowering me in battle. So yes, Bomani, we will have our fight, and I will hold the final piece of Ra's statue, just as I have foretold. It is simply a matter of when you would like to lose. If you would like to leave and return in a few years when you are more ready to die, I understand. But if you wish to behave like a man, you will begin your trek immediately. If you leave now you can be there in less than a day."

"What are you going to do? Walk alongside us and enter the tomb with me? Not a chance," Tommy scoffed.

Badru snarled. "Such a child. You are fortunate I leave your friends alive. But to kill them now would only make you act more irrationally."

"You're disgusting," Tommy said.

Badru's eyes narrowed and his face tightened with rage. "What did you say?"

"You're disgusting," Tommy stated again, factually. "Everything you do is based on fear. No one respects you, they only do what you say because they're worried you'll kill them. I'm not going to find the piece just because you say it's time."

"How dare you speak to me like this! I am the pharaoh!" Badru bellowed. The wind picked up again, pelting everyone with sharp grains of sand.

"Your *brother* was the pharaoh. You're nothing but a pathetic wannabe!" Tommy yelled back. The statue pieces warmed against his chest.

Though there were no clouds, lightning flashed suddenly through the sky and thunder shook the ground. "You will remove the final piece, as I have instructed you. And you will do it immediately! After the prophecy has been fulfilled, I shall rule all of Egypt and all of the heavens. Then I will punish Bastet for ever creating such an animal!"

Badru lifted his arm, revealing his three pieces in the palm of his hand. He pointed them at the unconscious bandit. The man began to distort and grow. His arms grew long and spindly, and more arms grew from his trunk to match them. His hands formed into gigantic pincers. His head shrunk back into his neck, and what looked like a log sprouted from his lower back.

The creature tested its new legs and scuttled side to side with renewed energy. Badru had changed the man into a gigantic scorpion.

Badru turned back to Tommy. "You will have the final piece for me by sundown tomorrow. For every hour that you are late, one of your friends will die." He pointed at Lily, who began floating in the air, flailing and screaming. A second later she snapped into silence and fell limply into Burt's arms. Badru moved his arm slightly to the side and did the same to Annie.

"These two are in a sleep from which they will not wake until they reach the ruins. This monster," he gestured to the scorpion, "will be my eyes. And if you do not know the way, you had better pray the gods take pity and reveal it to you. By tomorrow night my prophecy will be fulfilled. Be not afraid, Bomani, for you have no choice in this matter. Our destinies cannot be avoided."

And with that, he was gone.

CHAPTER 14

Tommy's Statement

Tommy continued to walk blindly backward, refusing to take his eyes from the enormous scorpion trailing too closely behind them. It was black as tar, shiny, and easily the most disgusting thing he had ever seen. It had no face, but Tommy swore it was smiling at him.

Tommy placed himself directly between the monster and his friends. If the scorpion attacked, he wanted it to know that it would have to go through him first.

Burt walked just ahead of him, next to Lily's camel. He held her hand and stroked her hair every time she made a murmur in her sleep. He hadn't spoken a word since they had left the ruins.

The camel carrying Annie's sleeping body walked just ahead of Burt, and beyond that, side-by-side, were the camels ridden by Asim and Masud.

Tommy didn't see any of this, but he knew it was there. They had been marching for hours. They were tired and hungry. And the sun was due to rise sometime in the next hour.

Tommy looked at the scorpion and a wave of hatred crashed over him. Tommy had no choice but to go where Badru told him and to be there when he was told to be there. He would remove the statue piece and fight a more refreshed, experienced, and vicious enemy until one of them was dead.

There was nothing Tommy could do to change that scenario. He felt completely helpless, and for Tommy there was no worse feeling in the world.

If he were to do something, it would have to be now. He had to show Badru that he wasn't helpless, that he would oppose him to the bitter end. He had to show he wouldn't be bullied.

Tommy looked at the scorpion and stopped walking.

The scorpion stopped as well. It waved its pincers and waited for Tommy to act.

Tommy shifted into a panther the size of a full-grown horse. His gray coat shimmered in the dying moonlight, and his hair bristled at the base of his neck. A deep growl started in his stomach and shook him to his paws.

He loosed a jungle roar that echoed for miles, smashing through the early morning desert silence. The scorpion shuffled back a step.

Tommy felt two large arms grab him around the neck, attempting to restrain him.

"Don't do this, Tommy. Please don't do this," Burt whispered in his ear.

Tommy looked to his friend and showed his teeth. He looked back to the scorpion.

Burt wheeled around to the front, putting himself between Tommy and the monstrous scorpion. He held up his hands.

"Please stop, Tommy. I know how you feel. But this isn't the answer. Killing him won't kill Badru," Burt said. As the earliest rays of the sun landed on them, Tommy noticed that his friend had tears in his eyes. He was scared.

"After we beat Badru, I'm more than willing to help you get rid of this thing. But now isn't the time. What if something happened to you while you were fighting? What if this makes you too tired to fight Badru? Or even too tired to get to the Abandoned City?"

Lily and Annie wouldn't ever wake up, Tommy thought. *That's what he's worried about. And he's right.*

Tommy looked at Burt, then stepped around him, until he was only feet from the scorpion. Again he let loose a mighty scream.

The scorpion stepped toward him and made quick half-jabs with its poisoned tail, but it did no more. Try as it might to hide it, Tommy had scared the beast.

Satisfied, Tommy walked to Burt and shifted back to his normal form. They hurried back up to the rest of the group. Tommy walked by Annie's side and held his cousin's limp hand. The scorpion continued to follow, but with a bit more distance between them.

At least that scorpion knows what it'll have to deal with eventually, Tommy thought. *At least it knows that.*

When the sun rose, Tommy and Burt had removed their shirts and placed them over Annie's and Lily's faces to protect them. They were now paying for their generosity. Both boys were bright red. The sun seemed to bounce off the sand like a mirror and cook them from every angle.

Tommy trudged through the desert lost in thought until Annie's hand squeezed against his. She pulled the T-shirt from her face with slow, clumsy movements.

"Tommy?" she asked. Her voice sounded like sandpaper. "What's going on?"

He didn't answer her immediately. His attention was set on the swirling sand in front of them, where shining buildings were rising like ghost ships from the desert floor.

It all appeared in just over a minute. One-story mud brick homes connected into long blocks. There were large water basins, small shops, and a market area full of vendor's wagons. Beautiful temples buttressed by tall, slender pillars arose. All of them as clean and bright as they must have been the day Bastet's storm arrived. All of them completely empty of life.

It was the Abandoned City.

It rose from the ground soundlessly, like a dream. Annie and Lily sat up and stared. Asim and Burt both ran to Tommy and clapped a hand on each of his shoulders. Masud just watched and laughed gleefully.

"A few thousand years ago, Tommy," Asim said, "this would all have been yours. Your family was loved here like no other before or since."

Tommy could feel the love, the familiarity, reaching out to him from every glistening brick and street. He suddenly felt a rush of calm flow through him.

Badru was wrong. He could have the desert, but this city belonged to the Bomanis. And it always would as long as Tommy had anything to say about it.

Something hissed behind him, and he turned to see the monster scorpion creeping closer.

"How are you feeling, girls?" Tommy asked Lily and Annie.

"A little confused, but you know . . . pretty good," Annie said.

Lily shrugged and nodded. Burt gently lifted her from her camel to the ground. Then he lent Annie a hand as she jumped down.

Tommy pointed his thumb back over his shoulder. "Well, our friend back there is politely reminding me that we have an epic battle to fight. Are you two up to it?"

"Oh, most definitely," Annie smiled devilishly.

"Masud?" Asim called out. "Do you know how to find the temple?"

The stocky old man dropped down from his camel and shrugged his shoulders. "I'm afraid the maps I've studied only get us this far. But if our ancestors were right, we don't really need maps anymore. Tommy, you think you can take it from here?"

Tommy nodded, growing more confident. "Yeah, I think I can."

CHAPTER 15

Homecoming

Tommy navigated through the empty streets like he had walked them every day of his life. He led them to the very center of town, to a lonely building with a billowing sun etched into the ground in front of it. It was a miniature pyramid, only two stories high, but it was easy to tell that it was special.

"The Pharaoh's Tomb," Burt said.

There were two beautiful wells placed on each side of the front entrance. They were full of a clear oil that burned a beautiful blue flame.

"Your ancestor's pharaoh was a great and humble man, Tommy," Asim said. "Instead of separating himself with an amazing temple in the desert, he directed that he be buried here. He wished to be near his loving subjects, in a tomb that would impress only those who knew what lay inside."

"The sun is about to go down," Lily said softly. She grabbed Burt's hand.

"Badru is going to be here soon. If he isn't already watching us," Annie said.

"Are you ready for this, Tom?" Burt asked.

"Of course he is." Masud smiled and winked.

Tommy looked to Asim.

"Of course he is," Asim said. "Tommy, the time has come to prove your own destiny. Don't let someone else's prophecy deny what you are truly meant to do. Succeed where all those before you have failed."

Tommy nodded and gave half a smile. He took a deep breath. "But before I go, I—"

"Afterward, Tommy," Asim interrupted. He put his hand on Tommy's shoulder. "For now, go do what you must do. We have more faith in you than you could ever know."

Tommy took another deep breath and let it out slowly. Then, he marched forward toward the tomb's only door.

Tommy barely pushed and the stone door swung inward. Two torches hung on either side of the doorway, and Tommy grabbed one. He dipped the tip in one of the flaming oil wells and it lit instantly. He turned and walked into the building, torch held high.

The door slid silently shut behind him.

Tommy's torch lit the corridor in front of him, but the darkness still impressed him. It felt like he had entered a completely different world in just a few steps. He pointed the torch gently in a circle around him and took in all that he could.

The room was beautiful. Tommy had expected gold and precious stones to cover every surface, but what he saw was even more impressive. Breathtaking carvings and paintings intertwined along the fifteen-foot-tall walls. Crocodiles, bulls, cats, dogs, and every other animal Tommy could imagine practically crawled out of their frozen images. People tilled their land and worshipped their gods, who accepted their offerings.

At the top of the center wall, framed by two tall pillars that reached to the ceiling, was the pharaoh. He sat upon his throne with both hands raised, raining joy down over his kingdom. Tommy recognized him instantly from his recurring dreams. The carving was amazing, so lifelike and accurate. But it was the man next to the pharaoh that held Tommy's attention.

To the right of the pharaoh was the most impressive warrior he had ever seen. He was standing firmly with his arms crossed upon his chest. His face was new to Tommy, but he had no doubt in his mind. That man was his ancestor. That was the first Bomani.

Tommy wished there was some way he could pay respect. So he held his breath, bowed his head, and made a silent promise to return Ra's statue to completion as quickly as he could, and to destroy Badru.

Satisfied, he turned to his left and started down one of the three available hallways. He was guided only by the feeling in his gut.

The first thing Tommy noticed about the dim, narrow hallway was that it wasn't anything like the insides of Egyptian pyramids he had seen in movies. There were no trapdoors, secret entrances, dummy hallways, or inscriptions that looked like curses. It seemed like the pharaoh had abandoned all fear of his tomb being defiled by raiders.

I guess you don't have to worry about grave robbers when your city is about to be buried under a sandstorm

and the only person capable of raising it is a descendent of your most loyal servant, Tommy thought.

The torch he held cast a gentle light, but he doubted he actually needed it. Even in pitch dark the gentle curves and even footing would have been easy to navigate. It was like the building wanted him to find the burial chamber.

Tommy could feel the hallway gradually winding deeper below ground. The air dropped a couple of degrees. Something in his stomach told him he was nearly there.

And then the doorway appeared before him.

To his right were the openings of the other two tunnels he could have taken. Tommy smiled. There was no wrong way to get to the burial chamber. It was all just a matter of which route you wanted to take.

Next to the heavy-looking stone door was an empty torch holster, and he placed his torch inside of it. He somehow had a feeling he wouldn't need it anymore. He nervously ran his hands through his long hair, then let out a quick breath and stepped forward. He put his hand on the door and pushed.

Visions

T he light from inside nearly blinded Tommy, but he stepped forward and his eyes gradually adapted. His head swirled, making him dizzy. The air inside the chamber was thinner and cooler, and a faraway buzzing filled his ears. He did his best to concentrate and looked around the tomb.

The pharaoh's treasure was stacked and layered around the floor, but Tommy ignored it. There was only one object he cared about, and he found it immediately. Against the far wall, perfectly centered and framed by piles of gold jewelry, was the pharaoh's stone coffin.

Tommy marched toward it, stepping over jewelry, precious stones, pottery, and gold-crusted weapons. The coffin was shaped roughly like a man laying on his back. It was rounded and thin at the top, then broad at the shoulders and tapered until it reached the feet. It was about seven feet long, three feet high, and looked like it was made of impossibly heavy yellow stone. It was beautiful.

Tommy stepped directly next to it and the buzzing in his head heightened.

On top of the coffin was a full-sized painting of the man inside. It was in exactly the same position he now rested, his arms crossed and eyes open and staring to the heavens.

On top of the painting was a simple crown. It was a band of gold holding just one stone directly in its middle.

Tommy grabbed the crown and his mind went blank. The buzzing stopped and was replaced with a thousand images, all flooding over him at once. They spoke to Tommy, told him stories and gave him warnings, and somehow he absorbed it all.

He watched an epic movie play in his head of generation after generation of Bomani warriors. They appeared first in Egypt and then every other corner of the globe, fighting back the dark waves of Badru's evil. They stormed castles, crawled through jungles, ran across sun-bleached beaches, and moved silently through shadows as they searched for the statue pieces.

The images showed Tommy how his ancestors had laid his bricks in fate's road. They showed him what it would take to accomplish what they were never able to.

And then they were gone.

The experience felt like it had taken years, but he knew it could only have been moments. He was back in the tomb, and the crown was in his hands. He was breathing heavily, but he didn't feel dizzy anymore. He felt powerful. He felt ready.

He gave a quick pinch and the final piece of Ra's sun statue fell from the crown and into his hand. He took a piece of gold wire from the ground and wrapped it tightly around the base. Then, he attached it to the others, enlarging his necklace.

Tommy turned and walked back to the open door. Before exiting, he stopped and slowly spun back around. He lowered his head and said a brief thank you to the pharaoh. Then he kneeled and grabbed a short, heavy sword from the ground.

Just in case, he thought.

Tommy walked back out into the hall and heard the door slide shut behind him. He knew it would never open again.

The first thing Tommy saw as he stepped out of the tomb was Annie. She had shifted, and her canine body was motionless on the ground.

Just past her Burt was yelling. "Don't even try to come closer!" He was swinging one of the tomb's lit torches like a baseball bat. The flames were warding off the gigantic scorpion, which shuffled side to side in an attempt to close in and attack.

Asim and Masud stood closest to Burt. They used their bodies to shield Lily from the danger in front of them.

"Your friends are not as good at dying as I had hoped, Bomani," Badru hissed. "The dog-girl was eager enough, but the others have proven more difficult."

Tommy raised his sword and Badru laughed.

Tommy looked at the sword and then at Badru. Badru stood in the street, highlighted by the last dying light of the day. Tommy knew this was no nightmare. This day had finally come.

"I have waited thousands of years for this day, and I never once thought you would cheapen it with a weapon," Badru said. "Respect our destinies, Bomani. Know that I am meant to destroy you, but fight me as our fates have intended."

Tommy thought for a second, then wheeled to the side and heaved the sword through the air. It skidded across the ground and landed at Burt's feet, who picked it up and held it in his other hand. He screamed with renewed vigor and swung both weapons as he forced the scorpion back. "I'm gonna need more help than that eventually, Tom!" Burt yelled.

"Ignore them," Badru said. "Their deaths are already determined. It is time to concentrate on yours."

Tommy nervously licked his lips. "How can you be so sure I'm the one who is going to die? How do you know your dream wasn't just a dream?"

Badru snarled. "Because for as long as I have lived I have seen only one thing every time my eyes closed: your cursed face in this inevitable battle. I have watched us duel more times than you could imagine in a dozen lifetimes. Every time I have seen myself hoist the seventh piece of Ra's statue. It is destined to be mine. And now it is time for the prophecy to be realized."

Tommy snuck a quick look at Burt. He was still keeping the scorpion at bay, but his swings were becoming labored. He couldn't go on much longer.

"I said to ignore them!" Badru bellowed. Thick veins bulged in his neck and on top of his bald head. "My waiting is over! Let us begin, so that the Bomanis may end!"

Tommy took a last look at his friends, then nodded.

"Let's do it," he said.

CHAPTER 17

Prophecy Fulfilled

I n the second before he shifted, Tommy felt an explosion of power burst from his necklace and through his body. He shifted into an enormous panther and roared. He wasn't any larger, but he could feel something was different. He charged Badru and leaped before he was halfway there, like a cannonball of dagger claws and teeth. He moved so quickly he couldn't believe it.

Unfortunately, so did Badru. He maneuvered easily to the side and Tommy didn't so much as touch his cloak. Badru shifted then into a large black dog. He had long, skinny legs, was barrel-chested, and had a pointed muzzle loaded with knife-sharp teeth.

They charged each other and collided like cars on a freeway. They rolled end over end, each snapping their teeth and jockeying for top position. Badru latched his teeth onto Tommy's leg and pain shot through Tommy's body. Tommy swiped his massive paw and took a chunk of flesh from the dog's rump, sending him skittering away.

Badru stopped and stared at Tommy. He clenched his teeth in an expression that almost looked like a smile. Suddenly a thick fog rolled through Tommy's brain and he felt nauseous. He looked at the wound on his leg and cried out in surprise. Mixed in with the blood was a murky brown liquid, thick and harsh-smelling.

Tommy looked again at the foam pouring from Badru's mouth and thought, *His teeth are venomous!* Tommy's heart began to pound. Had he already lost? Had he come all this way only to take a fatal blow in the first attack?

Tommy shook his head. He might be hurt, but he hadn't lost yet. However, he was going to have to act fast.

"Tommy!" He heard Burt yell. "I can't keep this thing off of us!"

But Tommy didn't have time to help. Badru charged again.

Tommy leaped to the side and narrowly avoided another poisonous bite. He sprinted away and set himself with his back to a temple. Now Badru was between him and the scorpion.

How can I help them if Badru keeps coming at me? he thought.

Quickly Tommy shifted into a tank-sized hippo and barreled toward Badru. Surprised, Badru tripped over himself to squeeze out of the way, but Tommy kept on running past him.

Tommy came up on the scorpion's rear, and using his powerful jaws, tore off the scorpion's tail. The scorpion instinctively leaped through the air, over Burt, and to the other side of Asim and the others. Burt chased after it before it could realize it had a clear shot at easier prey.

Tommy spun around just in time to see a massive crocodile running at him. He ran in a looping path around it, luring Badru away from his friends.

Badru wheeled around and smoothly changed into an incredible asp. He reared up with the top half of his body towering high above the ground and hissed.

Not sure what to do, Tommy shifted back into his normal form and sent a whirling blast of sand into the snake's eyes. Badru hissed again and thrashed around, temporarily blinded. He too shifted back to his normal form and fell to his knees as he tried to rub the sand from his eyes.

Tommy looked past him to Burt. The scorpion had regained its aggression and was slicing closer to Burt's head with every jab of its pincers. Burt looked tired. If Tommy couldn't put Badru down permanently, there wasn't anything he could do to help.

The poison from Badru's first bite sent a wave of nausea through him and his knees buckled. He fell to one knee, and his vision began to blur.

Then, emerging from behind a temple came someone Tommy had thought he would never see again. It was a skinny young boy, sunburned and limping, but sprinting as fast as his exhausted body would allow. With an impassioned scream, the boy tackled Badru to the ground.

Tommy nearly fainted.

"Now, Bomani!" Haji yelled. "Help your friends!"

Tommy looked at Burt. Burt had turned the scorpion to the entrance of the tomb, but he didn't look like he could fight much longer.

Using what felt like his last bits of energy, Tommy lifted his hands and concentrated. The oil from the flaming wells rose like geysers and dropped themselves on the scorpion's back. Burt threw his torch at the monster's back and ran. A great fiery ball rose into the sky, and there was nothing the scorpion could do. It took a couple haltering steps, then it fell to the ground and burned.

Badru stood up, tossing Haji into the air as he did. Haji landed with a sickening thud, and Badru was on him instantly. Roaring like a madman, he picked the boy up and threw him as if he were nothing but a sack of feathers.

Haji slid across the sandy floor and didn't stop until his body collided with a temple wall. Burt and the others ran to him, Burt kept the sword in case Badru followed.

But he didn't. Instead he turned to Tommy and pointed a long, crooked finger. "Enough!" he bellowed. "Enough with the games! I could have spilled your disgusting mixed blood the second you stepped from my brother's tomb. But I knew the prophecy demanded that we battle. And so you have fought, but for what?

"You ignored a chance to kill me while I was blinded to protect those vermin. You are weak! For generations your family has had the power to rule any land they wanted, to make themselves kings. Instead they needlessly battled me. Tonight it ends!"

Badru stood and pulled his statue pieces from a hidden pocket on the inside of his cloak. He held them in his palm and pointed them at Tommy.

"It is time for the prophecy to be fulfilled, and for my inevitable reign as pharaoh to begin."

Tommy also stood, though his knees wobbled. He could feel the venom pushing its way through his veins, trying to find his heart.

"I think it's time for a compromise, Badru," Tommy said. "You don't get to be emperor. But you can fulfill your prophecy."

"Silence! Your time to speak is over!" Badru growled. Tommy reached around his neck and removed the topmost statue piece, the one that had been in the pharaoh's crown.

As everyone watched in shock and confusion, he threw it to Badru, who caught it.

"Just like in your dream, Badru. You've got the seventh piece."

Badru looked at him curiously, but then his confusion faded and he began to laugh. He smiled and a dangerous light grew in his eyes.

"I . . . I can *feel* it!" he said. "The power is incredible!" His head snapped forward, and he looked to Tommy. "And soon I will have them all!"

With maniacal glee, Badru raised the four pieces and aimed them at Tommy. Tommy closed his eyes and dropped his chin to his chest.

Tommy spoke slowly, barely above a whisper. "I'm afraid not, Badru. You might kill me, but that would hardly be the end of your worries. You tried to control your fate by creating a prophecy. I'm controlling mine by making sure you understand that as long as you live, there will always be someone to fight you, no matter how powerful you may be."

Badru hesitated.

The sand began slowly swirling around Tommy's feet.

"Since you first tried to steal Ra's statue from your brother, you have been alone, living in the desert. You survived, and kept returning to bring pain to anyone brave enough to stand against you. When the fighting was done, you went back to your cave and waited for the next chance to spread evil."

Tommy's eyes stayed shut and his feet left the ground. He floated a few inches in the air with his hands at his side. His voice sounded different than usual, a bit older and deeper.

"And while you hid," he continued, "the Bomanis and their friends helped each other rebuild

105

and make stronger all that you had destroyed. Dozens of friends became hundreds and then thousands as people worked together to fight your evil. And tonight you're going to pay for what you've done to them. You're going to face each of them in turn."

Dark clouds rolled over the moon. Badru's arm lowered halfway and he took a step back.

"Even the whole statue wouldn't be strong enough to fight the storm of hatred you have brewed, Badru. Tonight, the storm has finally come."

Swirling gray smoke rose behind Tommy and spread. Then, it separated into individual shapes. Gradually the smoke morphed into people, until an army of beautiful dark-haired, dark-eyed Egyptian warriors stood behind Tommy.

Badru raised his four statue pieces in front of him. A dark swirl of gaseous energy balled in front of his fist and then blasted in Tommy's direction. In an instant, two of the ghost warriors weaved their way in front of Tommy and absorbed the blow.

Badru screamed in frustration and turned his aim to Tommy's friends. Before he could take a shot, the ghostly figures had formed a wall between them.

Badru staggered a step back and planted himself firmly on the ground. He put his hands together and smashed them into the ground like a mallet. The ground shook violently. Buildings began to fall away piece by piece, crashing to the ground. But Tommy didn't appear to notice.

"Your prophecy got you your seventh piece, Badru," Tommy said calmly. "But it isn't going to be enough to save you. Your evil is over."

Tommy raised his arms and on cue, the ghostly figures flew through the air toward their eternal enemy. They unleashed the deafening battle cries of four hundred defeated souls finally finding victory.

Badru kicked and punched and pushed, but it did nothing. The warriors twisted together in a tornado of writhing arms and legs, until Badru had disappeared into the ground, his screams swallowed by the desert sand. A sound rumbled up from below the ground, like a cannonball exploding.

The Abandoned City became silent.

And then Tommy collapsed.

CHAPTER 18

New Beginnings

Tommy woke in Haji's bed with the worst headache he had ever experienced. Every other inch of his body hurt as well.

He tried to sit up, but Mrs. Nasif gently pressed his shoulders back toward the bed. She shushed him soothingly.

Asim leaned into view. "It's okay. Let the boy sit if he'd like."

Tommy slowly pushed back up and swung his legs over the side of the bed. Everyone in the house was crammed into the small room and stood in a tight half-circle surrounding him.

"My apologies, Tommy." Asim smiled. "It seems my training wasn't as thorough as I had imagined. I neglected to mention that a poisonous bite is . . . *was* one of Badru's favorite and most dangerous tricks."

"So he's gone?"

Asim smiled and Tommy thought his old mentor was going to cry.

"Yes, Tommy. Yes indeed."

Annie sat down next to Tommy and put her right arm around him. Her left was in a sling, and she had a bruise on her forehead. "How you feeling, Cuz?"

Tommy thought about it. "Like going to a doctor probably wouldn't be a bad idea."

Masud laughed. "Give it a few minutes, Bomani. You've already got the best medicine the world can offer. Besides, we've called your mother and said you're fine. Going to the doctor would worry her." He smiled and pointed to the bed directly behind Tommy.

Lying on the mattress were all seven pieces of the statue.

"Burt found the rest," Lily said.

"Badru's pieces were on the ground where he disappeared," Burt said, shyly burning a hole in the floor with his eyes.

Everyone looked at Tommy as if they didn't know what to say next.

Neither did Tommy, but he gave it a try.

"Honestly, I don't know where all of that came from, either. When I was in the tomb, I realized that fighting Badru wasn't about me at all. If he had killed me, someone would have risen up to keep

109

fighting him. I guess all the pain and hatred he had caused for all those people over thousands of years just kind of funneled through me. I barely even knew what was going on."

"But you're still a hero, Bomani. Without you, Badru would be invincible. It wouldn't matter if a million of us rose against him. You saved the world."

Tommy looked up for the small voice that had spoken. Finally he found Haji, looking sheepish in the back of the room.

Tommy shook his head. "Nothing could have happened if you hadn't come back, Haji." He looked around the room. "Nothing could have happened without all of you. Which is why I'm separating the statue pieces amongst you. I'll keep my father's piece and the rest will go to Burt, Asim, Masud, Annie, Lily, and Haji."

The group gasped and looked at each other.

"But Tom, think of all the good you could do with the whole statue," Burt said.

"I'm not worried about me, Burt. I'm worried about others trying to take the statue for their own uses. The power, the temptation, would be too great. The pharaoh realized this. That's why he separated the pieces in the first place."

"But won't this create a new scramble for power? What of men like Fisk, who would risk anything to gain the entire statue?" Asim asked. "Are you sure you've thought this through, Tommy?"

Tommy took the pieces into his hands and nodded. "I have. And that is exactly why we must begin to rebuild the Protectorate, to strengthen it. The pieces and their locations must be kept secret, and we must do our best to keep them safe. This is our chance to give back to the people who have helped us for thousands of years."

"What about those of us in our, uh, later years?" Masud smiled. "I love an adventure, but I've probably only got so many left. What do I do when I meet the end of my road?"

Tommy shrugged. "Do like the pharaoh. Find someone far away you can trust. Someone you know will use your piece to make their world a better place. You'll know what's right."

He stood from the bed, still shaky from exhaustion, and handed each piece to its new owner. Burt thanked him and wiped a tear away. Lily's eyes sparkled. Annie jumped up and down with excitement. Haji took his piece with both hands, almost afraid to hold it. Masud winked at him, and Tommy winked back. Asim took his piece, hesitated, and then wrapped Tommy in a firm hug. Tommy hugged him back, and they held it until they were both laughing with joy and relief.

"It's over," Asim said, shaking his head. "I can't believe it's over. Your father would be so proud, Tommy. So proud."

"Just wait until we get home and start phase two. I've got all sorts of fun adventures in mind."

"Do we still get to take down bad guys?" Annie asked, eyebrows raised.

Tommy laughed. "Oh, most definitely. Trust me, by this time next year, we'll be living in a whole new world. Now it's up to us to make it that way. You guys up to it?"

The group hollered in agreement.

"Okay, then. Let's get to work."